W9-DCL-791

58

058

960

- 1960

63

5

SUKEY

ICE CREAM FOR TWO

STORY AND PICTURES BY
CLARE TURLAY NEWBERRY

HARPER & BROTHERS   NEW YORK

KEENE TEACHERS COLLEGE
LIBRARY

Personal
175

Juv
PZ
7
.N466
Ic
1953

OCLC # 1399508

ICE CREAM FOR TWO

Copyright, 1953, by Clare Turlay Newberry
Printed in the United States of America

All rights in this book are reserved. No part of the book may be used or
reproduced in any manner whatsoever without written permission except
in the case of brief quotations embodied in critical articles and reviews.
For information address Harper & Brothers, 49 East 33rd Street,
New York 16, N. Y.

Library of Congress catalogue card number: 53-7116

26220
3/16/54

To my son Stephen

ICE CREAM FOR TWO

CHAPTER ONE

One morning Bruce Fleming woke up, as usual, before his mother. He could see that her eyes were still closed, for her bed was only a few feet from his, across the small crowded room that served as living room, dining room, bedroom, and artist's studio.

He tried to lie still and not disturb her, but that was difficult for an eight-year-old boy who was wide awake and eager to begin the day. In his own room at home he had been able to make all the noise he wanted to without bothering anybody. Home was his grandmother's comfortable frame house in Portland, Oregon, where he and his mother had lived since his father died.

And home was a very different sort of place from the "furnished room with kitchen privileges" in New York City where they had spent the past two weeks.

At home there was a big yard to play in, with a swing and cherry trees. There was William, his grandmother's good gray tabby cat. And there were the kids next door to play with, and all his books and toys. Some books they had brought with them, of course—*The Jungle Book, Pinocchio,* and a few others— and such toys as would fit into their suitcases and steamer trunk. But most of his possessions had been left behind, along with his sled and bicycle. Worst of all, there was no place to play in New York except the lobby and roof garden of the apartment house in which they lived, for he was not allowed to play on the street. Bruce heaved a sigh. If only his mother had not wanted to come to New York and be an artist!

At last he could hold still no longer. He tumbled out of bed, leaned out of the window over the fire-escape, and stared up between the tall buildings.

"Mom!" he called. "Wake up! It's going to be a nice day— the sky is blue as anything. Mom, wake *up,* it's morning!"

His mother opened her eyes and glanced at the alarm clock on the bureau. "So it is," she said sleepily, reaching for her robe at the foot of the bed. She got up, opened the room door, and peered down the corridor.

"There's no one in the bathroom," she announced, "Better hurry, darling, and get that shower right now, while you have the chance. And, Bruce, do try to be quiet. It's Saturday, you know, and Miss Knapp and Miss Steele are still sleeping." Miss Knapp and Miss Steele were the two young women who shared the kitchen and bath with Bruce and his mother. Both of them were secretaries, and worked downtown during the week.

"Okay, Mom," said Bruce, and he galloped down the hall. In a moment, however, he was back. "Miss Knapp and Miss Steele are *not* still sleeping," he stated, "they're eating breakfast in the kitchen. So if you don't mind, I'm going to roar a little."

"Not at all," said his mother, and a few moments later he was under the shower, roaring happily.

By the time he was dressed breakfast was ready. His mother unfolded the card table and set it up in the middle of the room. Then she brought the oatmeal and other things in from the kitchen, while Bruce removed books, papers, and garments from the two chairs and drew them up to the table.

"What did you think of my roaring just now?" he asked, sitting down carefully, so as not to slosh his mother's coffee.

"Horrible, darling, simply horrible," said his mother politely, putting some bread in the electric toaster. He looked pleased.

"I was playing Prehistoric Animal," he explained. "Gosh, Mom, I sure do wish I had been a cave boy. Or an Indian before the White Man came. Wouldn't that be *perfect*?"

"It certainly would," his mother agreed. "Ouch! That's hot! Shall I butter it for you?"

"Yes, please . . . Because then I could live wild, like Mowgli in *The Jungle Book,* and have plenty of animals to play with. Mom, do you know what I'd do if we were rich?"

"Better eat your oatmeal before it gets cold . . . No, what would you do?"

"Well, first I'd buy me a great big farm out in the country, with a great big house on it. And there'd be a whole lot of big trees, with vines growing on them, to hold on to. And every morning I'd put on the cave-boy suit you made me, and then I'd practise jumping around in the trees. Then I'd put all the monkeys back in their cages—"

"All the *what*?"

"Monkeys. I forgot to tell you about that. I'd have a whole lot of monkeys to play with, to make it more like a jungle, you know. And then I'd have a pet puma cub. Two pet pumas, a girl puma and a boy puma. One for you and one for me. And they'd grow up and have babies, and pretty soon we'd have pumas all over the place. Wouldn't that be *perfect*?"

"Goodness, yes," said his mother. "Don't forget to drink your milk."

"Sure, sure," said Bruce, and obediently drained his glass. "Mom, when can we get a kitten?"

"Now, Bruce, I've told you over and over that we can't have pets in a place like this. There isn't room. When we have our own apartment, then we'll get a kitten."

"But when will that be?"

"Darling, I don't know. When I find some work. Pretty soon, I hope. Would you like another piece of toast?"

"Yes, please, if I can have jam on it . . . Well, I hope it isn't going to be much longer. Honest, Mom, we need a kitten. Without a kitten we live too sad, we have dull days. I'm lonesome here. I don't have any kids to play with."

"Oh, you'll soon meet other children. There are probably some right here in the building. And I'm sure to find work before long, and then we'll get our own apartment, and you shall have a kitten. You be a good boy while I'm downtown this morning," said his mother, gathering up the dishes, "I'll be back in time to get your lunch."

"Can I wear my cave-boy suit to play on the roof?"

"I suppose so. If you'll promise to come down and get your sweater if it's too chilly."

"Sure, sure."

"And, darling, try not to make a racket in the halls or down in the lobby. It bothers people."

"Okay, Mom, *okay*!"

CHAPTER TWO

The roof garden, luckily, had a high parapet, making it a safe place to play. With its flower boxes and garden furniture it was a pleasant spot, if not perhaps as jungle-y as Bruce might have wished, and in the April sunlight it was quite warm enough for his cave-boy suit. The cave-boy suit was new, made by his mother from some very convincing fur cloth, and he had a fine club to go with it, a stick with a rock tied to one end.

For a while he played happily and noisily by himself, dealing hostile "natives" and wild beasts many a telling blow with the club. Unfortunately an old lady in a deck chair was trying to take a nap, and his warfare proved too much for her, especially the howls of triumph that followed each victory.

"Little boy," she said at last, "if you don't stop that atrocious noise immediately I will go downstairs and report you to the management."

Bruce wasn't sure what would happen if he were "reported to the management," but he suspected it would be unpleasant. He said, "Okay, okay," in a subdued voice, and got as far away from her as possible, at the other end of the roof garden. Here he lay down at full length on the warm cement and closed his eyes. After that his lips moved and he waved his hands in the air, but he was as quiet as even a sleepy old lady could ask. He was deep in his favorite daydream now, the one about finding a dear little orphaned puma in the wilderness. He picked it up, and it began to purr . . .

"Rarr!" said something, right in his ear. Bruce jumped and looked up. Close beside him sat a very strange-looking animal, staring at him out of bright blue eyes. It was a sleek cream-colored beast with brown markings, and it wore a necklace of blue beads. Near it stood a little girl of about Bruce's age, watching him curiously.

"Hey!" said Bruce, sitting up. "What *is* this, anyhow? Is it a cat, or what?"

"Of course it's a cat," said the little girl. "What did you think it was?"

"I don't know," said Bruce rather stupidly. "It doesn't look like a regular cat, somehow. It looks more like some kind of an animal." He didn't mean this as an insult to the strange cat. He was thinking that it looked somewhat like a small puma, and the puma was his favorite animal. The little girl, however, did not know this.

"Sukey's a thoroughbred, pedigreed Siamese cat," she said indignantly, "and if she went to the cat show she'd take all the prizes. Daddy says so!"

"Huh!" said Bruce. "Just the same, she's an awfully funny-looking cat. She doesn't even sound like a cat." She didn't, either. Instead of saying *"me-ow,"* like a proper cat, she said *"rarr,"* way down in her throat. She sounded like a wild animal, but she didn't act a bit wild. She let Bruce stroke her soft fur, and bumped her head against him in the friendliest manner.

"She sounds like a Siamese cat," said the little girl fiercely. "And Siamese cats are the very best kind in the world!"

"That's what *you* say," remarked Bruce loftily.

"All right, you just watch, and I'll show you."

"Okay, go ahead and show me."

The little girl faced the cat. Patting herself on the stomach she repeated in a coaxing voice,

"Come on, Sukey, come on, Sukey, come on!"

Bruce had no idea what she was trying to do. While he was wondering about it, Sukey crouched low, gave a hoarse *"rarr,"* and sprang straight up into the little girl's arms.

"There," she said triumphantly, "I bet you never saw a cat that would do *that*, old Mr. Cave Man!"

"Maybe I have, and maybe I haven't," said Bruce grudgingly, but he ached with envy. To have a cat like that, one that looked and sounded like a jungle beast, and that would leap into your arms when you told it to! And to think that this treasure was wasted on a snooty girl!

"And now watch while I show you something else," said the little girl. She unhooked Sukey's claws from the front of her dress and set her down. Then she took a tiny red ball from her pocket. Sukey said, *"Rarr! Rarr!"* and waited eagerly. The little girl tossed the ball and the cat bounded after it.

Bruce started to say, "Aw, that's nothing. Any cat'll do that," when, to his surprise, Sukey trotted back with the ball in her mouth and dropped it proudly at their feet.

"Rarr!" she said, asking as plainly as could be for the ball to be thrown again.

"Jeepers!" cried Bruce. "How did you ever teach her to do those tricks? What else can she do? Let me throw the ball this time, will you?"

The little girl handed him the ball.

"Nobody taught her," she said, looking pleased. "She's just naturally smart. All Siamese cats are."

After that they took turns throwing the ball, until Sukey was so tired that she flopped down on the floor and refused to move. Bruce tried his best to get her to jump into his arms, repeating,

"Come on, Sukey, come on, Sukey, come on," in the most inviting tones, but it was no use. Sukey only blinked glassily at him and pretended not to understand.

"Say, do you live here? I never saw you before," said Bruce. He was beginning to think that this girl was not so bad after all. And Sukey was wonderful.

"Oh, I've been away for Easter vacation," said the little girl. "When there's no school I stay with my grandmother in Connecticut. My mother and my daddy both work, so there's no one at home to take care of me, except on Saturday and Sunday. Who takes care of you?"

"Oh, I take care of myself, mostly," said Bruce in rather a superior tone, "My mother goes downtown every day to see editors, and I just play up here on the roof, or down in the lobby, or else I stay at the Natural History Museum. Have you been there? It's super—all kinds of stuffed animals, and prehistoric bones, and *everything*."

"Don't you go to school?"

"Naw," said Bruce cheerfully, "I'm having a vacation until we find out if we're going to stay in New York. Boy, you sure are lucky to have a cat like Sukey." He sprawled on the floor beside the cat and tenderly smoothed her satiny fur. "Our cat at home—William—he's an awfully good cat, but he's not half as much fun as Sukey."

The little girl beamed.

"And she's not all," she bragged. "We've got Malo—he's the

WENDY AND POUNCE

father cat, and Wendy—she's the mother cat, and a little tiny new kitten that hasn't got its eyes open yet."

"Gosh! Can I see them?"

"I'll have to ask my mother," the little girl said primly. "She doesn't like to have children play with the cats."

Just then Anderson, the elevator boy, appeared on the roof.

"Oh, Bruce," he called, "your mother is home now, and she wants you to come down to lunch."

"Heck! I have to go now," said Bruce. "Okay, Anderson, I'm coming." He scrambled to his feet and ran to the elevator.

CHAPTER THREE

Mom!" he shouted, bursting into the little room where Mrs. Fleming was setting the table for lunch, "Mom, I was up on the roof, and there was a girl there, and she has the best cat! Some kind of a foreign cat, and its name is Sukey, and it does tricks! Gosh, I wish I had a cat like that!"

"I'm going to make French toast for lunch," said his mother, tying on an apron. "It will be ready in about two minutes, so go and wash quickly."

"Okay, okay," said Bruce, and he disappeared into the bathroom, muttering excitedly.

A few minutes later, with hands and face damply clean, he sat down to a plate of golden-brown French toast.

"That girl sure is lucky, isn't she, Mom?" he remarked, reaching for the syrup.

"Better let me pour that for you," said his mother quickly. "Syrup is awful to get out of things. . . . What girl?"

"Oh, Mom!" said Bruce. "You weren't even listening!"

"I'm sorry, dear, my mind was on something else. The girl with the nice cat, you mean."

"Of course. Isn't she lucky, Mom, to have all those cats?"

"I thought you said just one cat."

"No, she's got a whole lot of them, besides a little tiny kitten. So you see, Mom, you were wrong about people not being able to have cats here."

"I don't suppose those people live all in one room with their cats, Bruce. They probably have a whole apartment. Is the girl nice?"

"I guess so. Kind of snooty, though. But okay."

"How old? Just a little girl?"

"Oh, no. Quite big. About my size."

"What's her name?"

"Don't know," said Bruce, "but I sure hope she comes up on the roof again and brings that cat."

"I shouldn't worry about it, if I were you," said his mother comfortingly. "If she lives here in the building you are sure to see her again."

Bruce was insulted.

"Gosh, Mom," he said disgustedly, "it isn't *her* I want to see. It's the *cat*."

After lunch, Bruce, in too much of a hurry even to wait for the elevator, ran three flights upstairs to the roof garden. He looked all over it, but the little girl and her cat were gone. And they did not come back, although he waited until nearly dinner-time.

That evening, when he and his mother were eating dinner, the telephone rang in the hall. Mrs. Fleming answered it, and when she returned to the table she was smiling.

"Good news for you, Bruce," she said. "Your friend's name is Joanna Wiles, and her family, complete with Siamese cats, lives in apartment D4. You're invited to call on them this evening at seven-thirty, to meet the rest of the pussy-cats. "How's that?"

"Mom, that's wonderful," said Bruce. "But how do you suppose they found out my name? I never told her."

"That was easy. All they had to do was ask Anderson, 'What eight-year-old boy runs around the building dressed in a pair of sneakers and a leopard skin?' "

Bruce was in such a hurry to finish his dinner that he swallowed his milk the wrong way, and his mother had to thump him on the back to help him stop coughing. He watched the clock until it said two minutes before seven-thirty, and then raced down the stairs to apartment D4.

Joanna met him at the door and led him into the living room, where she introduced him to her father and mother.

"So this is the boy who likes cats," said Joanna's mother, with a smile.

As she spoke he heard a soft thud. Sukey had jumped down from a bookcase in the corner and was strolling toward him.

"*Rarr!*" she said, and bumped her head fondly against his bare leg. "See, she knows me!" cried Bruce with delight, rubbing his hand over her smooth tan fur.

"Sukey is our grandmother cat," said Joanna's father. "Young-looking for a grandmother, don't you think, Bruce?"

"Yes, sir," said Bruce shyly. Then he remembered how pleased his mother always seemed when anybody said how young she was to have such a big boy, and he added heartily, "She sure is!"

"And Malo, over there," said Mrs. Wiles, "is the father cat."

Bruce looked across the room and saw Malo sitting on the mantelpiece, with his tail hanging over the edge. He was larger than Sukey, and looked very dignified.

"Better not touch Malo," said Joanna's mother, as Bruce started toward him, "He doesn't know you yet, and he's rather shy with strangers. Let's go and see Wendy's new kitten."

The children followed her into a bedroom, and there, in a dark corner of the clothes closet, lay another cat like Sukey, beside the tiniest white kitten Bruce had ever seen. Its eyes were not yet open, and its fur was so soft and fine that the pink skin shone through it.

"Why doesn't he have a brown face and paws like the big cats?" asked Bruce.

"He will when he gets older," replied Joanna's mother. "Siamese kittens are born a creamy white. They get their dark 'points' later."

The mother cat, who had been lying down when they came in, was now half standing up, crouched over her baby. Although no one had touched either of them she began to growl. She seemed terribly afraid that something might happen to her kitten, and her eyes were so big and anxious that Bruce felt sorry for her.

"Is she cross?" he asked in a whisper.

"Not in the least," said Mrs. Wiles. "Wendy is a very sweet kitty, but she's nervous about her child. That's why we don't let people near her unless they are very fond of cats and know how to be gentle."

They went back into the living room so as not to bother poor Wendy any longer. There the children played with Sukey, while old Malo looked on scornfully from the mantelpiece. He was too dignified to play, but Sukey wasn't, for all that she was a grandmother, and she ran for the red ball again and again, and pounced delightedly at fingers wiggled under newspapers.

Then it was eight-thirty, Joanna's bedtime, and Bruce had to go home. But before he said good night, Joanna had promised to be up on the roof the next morning, as soon as she got home from Sunday School, and to bring Sukey with her.

CHAPTER FOUR

On Monday Joanna went back to school, and after that Bruce had to wait until evening to see her and the cats.

"I'd like to go to school, too, Mom," he said one morning at breakfast. "Why can't I?"

"Because, darling, we may not be in New York much longer," said his mother.

"You mean we're going home—back to Portland?"

"Perhaps. Would you like that?"

Bruce thought it over while he munched his toast.

"I don't know. Of course, I'd like to see Grandma and William, and I sure would like to have my bicycle, but I kind of like it here, too. I like the zoo, and the Natural History Museum, and I just love Joanna's cats. If we could have an apartment, like you said, and a kitten like Joanna's, I'd just as soon stay here."

"Well, I'm going to keep on trying to find work as long as our money holds out," his mother said. "Who knows—something may turn up any day. I'm going to see another editor this morning." She took her big portfolio under her arm, kissed Bruce goodbye, and set out.

The best part of the day was in the evening after dinner, for then Bruce was allowed to go to Joanna's apartment and see the kitten. It was thrilling to watch him grow. His blue eyes were open now, but he was still too little and weak to stand up. He could, however, crawl surprisingly fast. But mostly he just ate and slept, snuggled close to his warm mother. Bruce was careful not to touch him, much as he wanted to, and although Wendy remained watchful she no longer growled. She seemed to have decided that he was not so dangerous after all.

"Look, Mrs. Wiles," Bruce said one day, "the kitten has a little brownish smudge on his nose. And his ears are beginning to get dark along the edges."

"Of course," said Joanna's mother. "He is beginning to get his 'points,' like a proper Siamese cat. He'll keep on getting browner and browner, the older he grows, like a piece of bread being toasted."

Another thing Bruce noticed about the kitten was the way

his ears were growing. At first they had been so tiny you could hardly see them, but now they appeared to be growing much faster than the rest of him. Bruce longed to play with him, but that was forbidden, for he was still too little.

Old Malo was becoming friendlier, too, and would sometimes leap down from the bookcase or mantel and saunter to meet Bruce when he came to the apartment. He would sniff Bruce's outstretched hand and allow his head to be rubbed, but he never wanted to be picked up. Sukey loved to be picked up and carried about, but to Bruce's great disappointment she still refused to spring into his arms.

"You'll have to wait until she knows you better," said Joanna's mother. "And you mustn't be so anxious for her to jump. Cats hate to be made to do anything. You have to act as if you didn't care whether she jumped or not."

So Bruce tried. He patted his stomach just as Joanna did, and called "Come on, Sukey, come on, Sukey, come on," in what was meant to be an unconcerned manner. But Sukey saw through him and refused to jump.

Then, one evening when he went to the Wiles' apartment, Sukey raced across the living room and landed on his shoulder, almost knocking him down. Her sharp claws went right through his thin polo shirt and dug into his flesh, but he didn't mind a bit. He would gladly have suffered more than that for such a welcome from Sukey. After that, to his delight, she often greeted him in this fashion, and sometimes even jumped into his arms when he asked her to.

"You know something, Mom? I'd rather have a Siamese kitten like Joanna's than anything," he told his mother one night at bedtime.

"Even more than a puma cub?"

"Yes," said Bruce firmly, "even more than a puma cub. Because Siamese cats are just as pretty as pumas, and they look just as wild, only they aren't. They're tamer, even, than regular cats, and they're smarter, and more fun to play with."

"I'm glad to hear it," said his mother. "Not that I don't admire pumas, but I doubt if they'd be cosy to keep in a small apartment. I'd far rather you went in for Siamese cats."

"Mom," said Bruce seriously, "you know Joanna's family has got all those nice cats—do you suppose they want to keep the kitten, too? I do so want him."

"Honey, I'm sorry, but you mustn't even think of it. And you certainly mustn't hint about it to Joanna or her parents. Cats like that are very expensive. People don't give them away—they sell them."

This was a blow. It had never occurred to Bruce that kittens were bought and sold.

"How much would one cost?" he asked in a small voice.

"I don't know exactly. Forty or fifty dollars, I suppose. Or even more."

Bruce whistled.

"*Whee!*"

"But never mind. One of these days you shall have a nice kitten of your own, even if it isn't a pedigreed Siamese. And you'll like it every bit as much as you do Joanna's kitten."

"Maybe," said Bruce sadly.

CHAPTER FIVE

Bruce looked forward to the week ends, for then Joanna would be home for two days, and they could play with Sukey on the roof. One Saturday morning immediately after breakfast, he was in the roof garden, waiting for her. This time she was late, and when she did appear the cat was not with her. She walked slowly toward him, and he saw that she had been crying.

"Hi, Joanna," he said. "Where's Sukey?"

Joanna did not answer. She sat down on a bench and stared out over the city, just as if she were alone.

Bruce looked at her uneasily. Then he tried again.

"How's the kitten?"

Joanna was silent.

"I said, 'How's the kitten?'" cried Bruce angrily. "I should think you could answer a simple question!"

For answer Joanna burst into tears.

"Gosh, Joanna, what's the matter?" said Bruce. "I didn't mean to make you cry."

Then Joanna began to talk, but as she was crying at the same time she was rather hard to understand. The kitten, she sobbed, was going to die.

Bruce was appalled.

"But why? Can't he have a doctor if he's sick?"

"He isn't sick," wept Joanna. "He's going to starve to death." She explained that Wendy, the mother cat, no longer had milk to give the kitten.

"Then why don't you give him some milk in a dish?"

"He can't drink it that way. He's too little."

She went on to say that a kitten so tiny would have to be fed with a medicine-dropper every two or three hours, night and day, if its life were to be saved. And there was no one to do this, for both her parents worked downtown all day, and she went to school.

While she was talking a wonderful idea came to Bruce.

"Joanna, listen. Why couldn't my mother and I take care of the kitten and feed him, until he is old enough to drink milk by himself?"

Joanna's tear-stained face lighted up with hope.

"But would she?"

"I bet she would! My mother loves kittens just the way I do. I'm almost sure she would."

"Go ask her right now," urged Joanna, "and I'll go and tell my mother."

"Okay!" And the two children tore across the roof and clattered down the stairs.

"Mom, Mom!" shouted Bruce, bursting into their room, where his mother was at work over her drawing-board, "Listen, Mom! Would you take care of Joanna's kitten and feed him with a medicine-dropper? Because if you don't he's going to starve. Will you, Mom, will you?"

His mother laid down her pencil and turned to look at him.

"What on earth are you talking about, Bruce? Why should I take care of Joanna's kitten?"

"It's like this," explained Bruce, stammering a little in his excitement. "Wendy—that's the mother cat—she can't feed the kitten any more. And he's too little to lap milk out of a dish. You have to feed him with a medicine-dropper, so—"

"But why," interrupted his mother, looking baffled, "am I chosen for this job? Why can't the Wiles family feed their own kitten, for heaven's sake?"

"Oh, Mom, you don't understand! They *can't!*" said Bruce, almost in tears. "Joanna's mother and father work downtown all day, and she goes to school, and you have to feed the baby kitten real often, or he'll die. Will you, Mom, *will* you?"

"But how can I say? Does Mrs. Wiles want me to take care of her kitten?"

Before he could reply there was a light knock on the door. It was Joanna, her face newly washed and smiling.

"My mother says if you want to take the kitten right now, Mrs. Fleming," she announced, "you can have him to keep."

Bruce gave an ear-splitting yelp of joy, then stopped and looked questioningly at his mother.

"But I thought that Siamese cats were very valuable," said Mrs. Fleming. "Are you sure, Joanna, that your mother wants to give the kitten away?"

"Oh, yes, Mrs. Fleming," Joanna assured her, "because if you don't take him he'll die. Mother says so."

"See, Mom, I told you!" cried Bruce, hugging himself to keep from bursting with excitement.

"But where would we keep him?" his mother objected. "There isn't an inch of extra space here."

"But he's so little—he won't take up any room at all. Oh, Mom, you aren't going to say we can't!" wailed Bruce, his eyes filling with tears.

"I don't know what to say," murmured his mother, surveying the little crowded room. Her worktable, beside Bruce's bed, was heaped with drawing-pads, portfolios, books, pencils, brushes, bottles, and paint rags. Bruce's cot had books and toys crammed under it and piled on top of it. Under her own bed were boxes and suitcases, and on it, books, newspapers, magazines, and more toys. The one clothes closet was so jam-packed with their belongings that you had to open the door very gently, or things fell out on you.

"Well, I suppose I'd better look for a box to put him in," she said at last, and the two children shrieked with joy. Joanna scurried back to her mother, who called Mrs. Fleming on the phone a few minutes later. The two mothers had a long conversation, and when Mrs. Fleming hung up she turned to Bruce and said,

"Joanna was right—they really do want to give us the kitten. But there is something you must try to understand, Bruce. Mrs. Wiles says the kitten may not live."

"Why not, if we feed him?" asked Bruce, startled.

"Because he's such a tiny kitten, only two weeks old, and Mrs. Wiles thinks the mother cat's milk must have dried up gradually, so that the kitten probably hasn't had enough to eat for several days. He may be too weak to save now."

Bruce looked solemn when he heard this, but he couldn't stay depressed long. Not when he was to have the kitten for his very own, the kitten he had longed for. He just couldn't believe it would die.

CHAPTER SIX

At the Wiles' apartment Joanna's mother told Mrs. Fleming how to mix a formula for the kitten, and gave her a medicine-dropper and a can of powdered baby food. Then Mrs. Wiles wrapped the kitten in one of Joanna's old doll blankets, with just his little nose showing, and handed him to Mrs. Fleming.

"Don't let him get chilled, whatever you do," she cautioned. "And you'd better feed him every two hours, night and day, for the next two days, at least. After that, every three hours during the day, and one night feeding should be enough."

And now poor Wendy, seeing her child taken away from her, began to cry pitifully.

"We'll take good care of your kitten, Wendy," Bruce assured her. "I do wish we could explain everything to her, so she won't worry," he added.

"Never mind," said his mother, "we'll bring the kitten back to see her when he's older, and then she'll know he's all right." She promised to follow Mrs. Wiles' instructions faithfully, and to call her on the telephone if she needed more advice. Then Bruce and his mother hurried back to their own room with the precious kitten.

"Let me hold him, Mom, please, let me," Bruce begged. "I never have held him yet."

"All right, you take him while I mix his formula. Don't let him out of the blanket, though, or he'll get cold."

So Bruce tenderly held the bundled-up kitten in his arms, while his mother mixed the powdered baby food with milk and warmed it on the gas stove. All this while the kitten had been uttering small plaintive sounds that wrung their hearts. They both felt that he might die at any moment if he were not fed very soon indeed. So it was a surprise to find that the starving infant did not want to take the formula from a medicine-dropper.

Mrs. Fleming tried repeatedly to get the tip of the dropper into his tiny mouth, but each time he clamped his jaws shut and shook his little head—*no*! She managed to dribble milk on his blanket, her dress, and the kitchen floor, but she could not get any of it inside the kitten.

"I'm afraid this just isn't going to work," she said unhappily, and Bruce wailed, "Oh, Mom, it's *got* to!"

At that moment Joanna knocked on the door. "Look what I found in my toy box!" she cried, and she held out a doll's nursing bottle. "Mother says to try it—it might work better than the medicine-dropper."

By this time the milk was cold, so Bruce's mother warmed it again. Then she filled the little nursing bottle and offered it to the kitten. Again he clamped his jaws shut and shook his head. But she kept on trying, and finally he grew tired of dodging. He opened his mouth in a mew of protest and she popped the nipple into it. Much against his will he swallowed a drop or two of warm milk. All at once he quit struggling. Why, this was food! He began to drink eagerly, with loud smacking noises, ecstatically kneading the air with his tiny forepaws.

Joanna, Bruce, and his mother all drew long breaths and smiled with relief as the kitten drained the little bottle.

"There, that's enough for this time," said Mrs. Fleming triumphantly. "We'll give him more later. In the meantime we'll fix his bed."

The bed was a brown paper carton from the grocery store, and when it was lined with a piece of soft blanket it made a deep cosy nest. They put the kitten in it and set it beside the radiator in their room, where it would keep nice and warm. Joanna's mother now phoned for her to come home, as they were going shopping, but Bruce scarcely left the kitten's side for the rest of the day. He even insisted upon eating his meals sitting on the floor, where he could gaze adoringly into the box.

The next morning when Bruce awoke he found his mother sitting on the floor in her robe and pajamas, feeding the kitten. The kitten was smacking his mouth over his bottle and kneading the air contentedly, but Mrs. Fleming looked tired and cross.

"Oh, Mom, let me feed him—I know how!" he begged, holding out his arms.

Without looking up his mother said crossly, "Bruce Fleming, you get yourself washed and dressed, and don't bother me!"

"Okay, okay," murmured Bruce, wondering how anyone with a brand-new Siamese kitten could possibly be in a bad humor.

"Seems to me you're not in a very good mood this morning," he ventured.

"Good mood, hah!" snapped his mother. "You wouldn't be in a good mood either, if you'd been up all night with this cat!"

Bruce thought privately that it would be grand fun, but he was too wise to say so.

"Every two hours I fed him," grumbled his mother, "*Every two hours*, all night long! Why I ever let myself in for such a job I don't know. I must have been out of my mind."

Bruce wasn't really listening. For some reason his mother was cross this morning, but grown people were often like that. She'd

MALO, WENDY, AND POUNCE

probably be all right when she'd had her coffee. He was watching the kitten.

"He's not going to die, like Joanna's mother said, is he, Mom?"

"Well, he's eating more this morning than he did yesterday," said Mrs. Fleming in a more cheerful tone of voice. "And he seems livelier. I really think he's going to be all right." At this point the kitten refused more food and she held him up against her shoulder, patting him softly. Suddenly she gave an exclamation of delight. "Bruce, guess what! The little darling is actually purring!" She held the bundle of kitten against Bruce's ear.

"He *is* purring—I can hear him! Oh, Mom, do let me hold him!"

His mother handed him the kitten and they both gazed raptly at the little creature.

"Oh, Mom, isn't he *cute*!"

"He's adorable," murmured his mother, forgetting all about her sleepless night. "And do you know, he reminds me quite a bit of you, when I first knew you. Only *his* ears are different, and, of course, *you* didn't have whiskers!"

CHAPTER SEVEN

For the next week Bruce's mother got very little sleep, and she complained bitterly about it. She frequently remarked that no one in her right mind would think of going to so much trouble for a cat. She kept on, however, according to Mrs. Wiles' instructions, and Pounce, as they named the kitten, grew steadily bigger and livelier. Presently he was old enough to get through the night with only one feeding, and soon after that he slept all night without being fed at all, and had his bottle only in the daytime. Then the worst was over, and Mrs. Fleming was able to catch up on her sleep. And by the time he was a month old he was eating ground beef and lapping milk out of a saucer like a grown-up cat.

When Pounce was six weeks old they took him to the Wiles' apartment to call on his family. Bruce thought Wendy would be overjoyed to be reunited with her son, but she took it very calmly. She sniffed him all over, gave him a casual lick or two, and walked off with her tail in the air. Malo and Sukey were, if possible, even less interested. "I don't believe they even remember him," said Bruce, rather shocked.

One afternoon his mother came home looking very happy.

"Bruce, what do you think?" she cried, throwing down her bag and portfolio. "I've found some work at last! Six designs for children's stationery. What do you think of that?"

"Swell," said Bruce absent-mindedly from the floor, where he was building a fort for Pounce out of the bed pillows and his mother's drawing-board.

"It certainly *is* swell," said his mother. "I was just about ready to give up and go back to Portland."

Bruce sat up on his heels. "Are we going back to Portland?"

"Not if I can get enough work here," his mother replied cheerfully, "and I think I can now. If I can get one job like this I can get others."

Bruce looked thoughtful. "Supposing we did go back, Mom, could we take Pounce?"

"Now, Bruce, you know we couldn't. I told you that when we got him. No, we'd just have to give him back to Joanna. A tiny kitten like that would surely die on such a long journey. Besides, they wouldn't let us take him on the bus."

Bruce picked Pounce up and held the warm purring little body against his cheek. "I wish I could make some money," he said earnestly. "If I could catch some robber and get a reward, then we could stay here all right and keep Pounce."

"I don't think you're very likely to catch any robbers, darling, but there is something you can do that will help a great deal."

"What?"

"You can pose for these drawings I have to make. I'm going to do them just as well as I possibly can, so that these people will want me to do more work for them, and I'll need you for a model. I'll need a little girl model, too, so if Joanna will pose it will be wonderful."

"Of course I'll pose, Mom," said Bruce eagerly. "And I'll really hold still this time, and not wiggle the way I used to when I was little. And I'll get Joanna to pose, too."

Joanna, fortunately, was delighted with the idea of being an artist's model, and Bruce's mother made many sketches of the two children. Posing, of course, wasn't as much fun as they had thought it would be. They got "pins and needles" in their arms and legs, and it was surprisingly difficult to hold still for more than a few seconds. But they did as well as they could, and Mrs. Fleming told them stories as she drew, to make it easier for them. When she had made all the studies she wanted she gave several of the drawings to Joanna, to take home to her parents.

For the next week Bruce's mother worked long hours on the six water-color drawings. Bruce did all he could to help. He was as good as he knew how to be. He went to bed the minute he was told, instead of arguing about it. He washed his hands and face really clean before coming to the table. He ran errands to the corner grocery, and dried dishes, and kept Pounce up on the roof as much as possible, so the playful kitten could not bother his mother at her work.

For Pounce was beginning to live up to his name. He pounced at everything. He knocked Mrs. Fleming's pencils and erasers off the table, whenever he had a chance, and hid them under the rug, where they were hard to find. He untied Bruce's shoelaces when he was reading, and one night he ate quite a large hole in the sleeve of Mrs. Fleming's best sweater. When she was drawing he bothered her dreadfully by leaping at her pencil as it moved across the paper. He loved to tear up paper, any kind of paper, and he left little toothmarks along the edges of all their books and magazines. In short, he was a nuisance, and Mrs. Fleming was very glad to have him stay up on the roof with Bruce while she completed her delicate little drawings.

At last they were finished.

"Gosh, Mom," Bruce said, gazing at them, "you sure do draw swell!"

There were six water-color drawings in gay colors: three of little girls playing with dolls and doll buggies, and three of little boys playing with toy trains and sailboats.

"Thank you, Bruce. I think they look pretty nice, myself," said his mother. "And now I'll take them downtown and get my money. There's plenty of time to make it before the place closes."

"How much money will you get?"

"Thirty dollars, five for each drawing," replied his mother, putting them carefully into a portfolio.

"Whee! That's a lot, isn't it?"

"Well—it should be more, really, but I hate to haggle. And we're so low on cash that even thirty dollars sounded pretty good to me. I'll be home as soon as I can, and we'll celebrate. We'll have ice cream for dinner," said his mother gaily, and she hurried off with the drawings under her arm.

CHAPTER EIGHT

I t seemed a very long time to Bruce, waiting for his mother to return with the promised ice cream. He hoped she would bring a lot of it, and that it would be chocolate. There had not been any ice cream for him lately, or much dessert of any kind, for that matter. That was because his mother had been too busy to bother about it, he supposed.

He was lying on his bed, reading *The Story of Dr. Dolittle*, with Pounce curled up beside him, when his mother came in. She looked hot and tired.

"Well, did you get it?" he demanded, meaning both the money and the ice cream.

She did not answer at once. Taking a pencil from her work-table she went to the closet door, where she had thumb-tacked a sheet of paper upon which to keep an account of the money they spent. On it she wrote, "Subway fare—20¢."

"No," she said wearily, "the woman who ordered the draw-ings wasn't there. I left them with her secretary. *She* said her boss would be back before closing, and if the stuff was all right there'd be a check for me in the mail tomorrow morning."

"Aw, heck!" grumbled Bruce, "I suppose that means no ice cream for dinner. Mom, you promised to get ice cream." His mother didn't answer. She put on her apron and went into the kitchen. A few minutes later they sat down to dinner, while Pounce lapped milk and pablum under the table.

When Bruce saw his plate he uttered a howl of indignation. It was bad enough to miss out on the ice cream he had been look-ing forward to all afternoon—but *mush* for dinner!

"Aw, heck, Mom, I don't want mush! I already had it this morning for breakfast, and I never did like it, anyhow. It isn't fair to make me eat it for dinner, too!"

"Nonsense," said his mother, sipping her tea. "Lots of people never have anything more exciting to eat than mush. Don't you know how in books they are always sitting down to a simple bowl of porridge?"

"Huh!" said Bruce, unimpressed. Scowling, he poured milk over the cereal, and sugared it as heavily as he dared.

"And in *Heidi*," continued his mother, warming to her

MALO

theme, "they lived on goat's milk, and black bread, spread with golden-yellow toasted cheese. Somehow that always sounded awfully good to me."

"Well, it may sound awfully good to you, Mom," said Bruce bitterly, "but it sure doesn't sound awfully good to me. What sounds good to me is ice cream, and strawberry shortcake, and peach pie, and chocolate cake, and ice cream, and all kinds of stuff like that."

"There is something in what you say," his mother admitted. "Only my choice would be a thick, rare sirloin steak, with French-fried potatoes. And apple pie à la mode for dessert. However, according to the package, this mush is the perfect diet —simply swarming with vitamins. At any rate, it's filling."

For awhile Bruce ate reluctantly. Presently he brightened.

"What do you say, Mom, we play we're a couple of Mounties, and we're lost up in the North Woods, and our grub supply is running low?"

"Indeed it is running low, pardner," said his mother, "and we're snowed in, besides. If help doesn't come soon, all will be lost. We're on our last piece of venison now, and by the look of things, pardner, our next meal will be your boots."

"My *boots*!"

"Certainly. That's what they always eat in stories, when all else fails. I mean, after they've already eaten the pack dogs, of course. What we're gnawing on now is probably the tail end of the last husky. Your sneakers are about worn out anyway, pard-ner, so why not eat 'em?"

"I don't think I'd like them, pardner," objected Bruce squeamishly. He wondered what rubber and canvas really would taste like.

"Sure you would," insisted the other Mountie, with horrid glee, "if only you got hungry enough. With quite a lot of salt and pepper they'd be delicious, and a nice change for us. Don't be fussy, pard."

"What's that outside the cabin?" demanded Bruce, hoping to get away from the subject of his boots. Shielding his eyes from the snow's glare he peered out of the window at the next apart-ment house. "Is it a friend, come to rescue us from our sad plight?"

"Certainly not," scoffed his mother. "What's the matter with your eyes, pardner? Can't you see that's our worst enemy, come to gloat over our discomfiture—or worse—the low-down, no-account, sneaking horse-thief! Well, pardner, it's him or us this time. Do you want to shoot him, or shall I?"

"Oh, please, Mom—I mean pardner—let me do it! You know I'm the best shot in the whole Northwest. *Pow! Pow!* Got him!"

"Neatly done, pardner. I couldn't have done better myself, even if I *am* the best shot in the entire North. And now that the base wretch is rubbed out, and considering how low our grub supply is—let's be practical, pardner—let's eat him."

Bruce was horrified.

"Oh, *no*, Mom! Let's skip that part, *please!*" Then he rallied. "What! Eat that black-hearted scoundrel? I'd die first!"

At that they both burst out laughing.

"Never mind, honey," said his mother, "if that check comes tomorrow—and I don't see why it shouldn't—I promise you'll have your ice cream. And we'll go to the movies, too. We'll really celebrate. For once, you shall have all the ice cream you want."

26220

KEENE TEACHERS COLLEGE
LIBRARY

CHAPTER NINE

Every morning Pounce awakened Bruce. He would leap upon the boy's stomach and stand there, prancing and purring and kneading with his paws—"making bread," Bruce's mother called it. If Bruce didn't open his eyes Pounce tried other tactics. He would sniff all over Bruce's face, then delicately lick his eyelashes. This tickled so much that Bruce would wake up laughing.

But Pounce didn't have to bother this morning, for Bruce was awake before he was. For this was the day of the promised movie and ice cream.

Bruce rolled out of bed and ran to the hall door to see if

Anderson had left any mail. A moment later he galloped back, waving an envelope and shouting,

"Mom! Mom! Here it is! Hurry up and open it!"

His mother quickly sat up in bed, reached for the envelope, and tore it open. Bruce watched her face as she scanned the narrow slip of paper that was inside. When she didn't say anything he hopped up and down with impatience.

"What's the matter, Mom? Isn't that it? Isn't that the check for thirty dollars?"

His mother stared at the check in her hand. After a pause she said, "It's the check, all right." Her voice sounded funny, as if she found it difficult to speak. "Only . . . it isn't for thirty dollars. It's for five."

She went on, as though thinking aloud, "It *must* be a mistake. This just *can't* be right."

"Did the lady *say* thirty dollars, Mom?"

"Why, yes, of course she did. I'm sure she did . . . No, I'm not . . . I remember now. She said, 'I'd like five or six drawings. I can afford to pay five dollars for some drawings like that.' . . . That's it. It isn't a mistake. She meant five dollars for *all* the drawings. I thought she meant five dollars *apiece*."

"Then—does that mean we can't go to the movie, or have ice cream after all? Mom, you promised. You said I could have all the ice cream I wanted. You *promised*. And I never have had all I wanted in my whole life!"

Suddenly his mother laughed.

"Of course we'll go to our movie and have our ice cream," she said, but her voice still sounded strange. "We've got five dollars, haven't we? That should buy a lot of ice cream."

"You mean it?"

"Certainly I mean it. Hurry now and get dressed, because we're going out to breakfast this morning. No mush for us today. You can have anything you like."

For once Bruce did not dawdle over his dressing, nor did he lapse into one of his frequent dream-states. And all Pounce's attempts to play were sternly rebuffed. When they were ready to go they locked Pounce in the room with enough food for two meals, in case they didn't get home for lunch. Then they went down in the elevator, stopping at the office on the way out to cash the check for five dollars.

It was only a short walk to Schrafft's restaurant, and presently Bruce was following his mother past the candy counter and soda fountain to the tables in the rear. There they sat down at a little glass-covered table with lace-paper doilies on it. A waitress in a starched white apron gave them each a breakfast menu, then stood before them, a pad and pencil in her hands.

"Can I really have anything I want?" asked Bruce.

"Well . . . anything within reason," replied his mother. "Better not order anything like nightingales' tongues, though, or poached dinosaur eggs."

Bruce did not smile. He was studying the menu with frowning concentration. It would be dreadful to order one thing, and then find that what you really wanted was something else altogether.

"Orange juice, grapefruit, stewed prunes, baked apple," he read silently, his lips moving, "cereal, toast, rolls, muffins. Eggs—boiled, poached, fried, or scrambled. Ham, bacon." He had thought that going out to breakfast would be a great treat, but all this sounded very much like what he was used to at home.

"Well, Bruce, what do you want?" his mother said at last, feeling that they simply must not keep the waitress standing there any longer.

Bruce darted his mother a quick look from under his lashes. He took a deep breath and said daringly,

"What I'd *really* like, Mom, is a nice big chocolate ice cream soda!"

To his surprise his mother took this calmly.

"Very well," she said, and she turned to the waitress. "A chocolate ice cream soda for the boy, please, and I'll have apple pie à la mode and coffee."

"Yes, miss," said the waitress in a bored voice. What did she care whether people ate properly or not? She wrote down the order on her little pad, and whisked off to give it to the young man at the soda fountain.

"Now this is the kind of breakfast I'd like to eat every day," sighed Bruce, when the last delicious drop of chocolate syrup had been drawn protestingly up the straw into his mouth.

"Me, too," said his mother dreamily. She swallowed her last

bite of apple pie and ice cream, and finished her coffee, then opened her handbag and replaced some of the lipstick she had eaten with her breakfast. "Wipe off your brown mustache, darling, and we'll be on our way to the movies. There's a good show at the Music Hall this week—would you like to go there?"

"Sure," said Bruce, "that sounds okay."

The morning rush hour was almost over, but there were still quite a lot of people on the subway platform, waiting for trains to carry them downtown to their jobs. Bruce's mother held his hand tightly, as she always did in the subway, so as not to lose him in the crowd.

Soon the downtown express came thundering into the station and roared to a stop. All the heavy doors slid open, to let the inside people out, and the outside people in. Everybody hurried as fast as they could, to get where they wanted to be before the doors closed. For, once closed, they would not open again until the next stop. Bruce's mother pushed him ahead of her into one of the cars just in time, and the big doors closed swiftly behind them.

They were scarcely seated when he clutched his mother's arm and pointed to an advertising placard above the window opposite.

"Look! It says International Exhibition of Snakes! Admission 50¢. Children 25¢. Oh, Mom, *could* we—"

"I thought you wanted to go to a movie."

"I did, Mom, but I'd much rather see the snakes."

POUNCE

"Oh, dear, would you, really? Are you sure, Bruce? It's been such a long time since I've seen a good show. Don't you remember how much you liked the Music Hall that time we went— the nice squashy seats, and the Rockettes all dancing in a row, and everything?"

"The Music Hall is okay, Mom," he explained patiently, "and the Rockettes are okay, too. But just the same, I'd an awful lot rather see the snakes."

His mother sighed. "All right, darling, snakes it is."

And snakes it was, indeed.

CHAPTER TEN

It was too bad that his mother didn't like snakes, thought Bruce, as he leaned his elbows on the wooden railing and gazed tenderly at a huge coiled python in a wire-covered box. But she had refused to look at any of them, even the two-headed turtle, which wasn't, of course, a snake at all. She said they made her stomach turn over, so she sat at the far end of the exhibition room on a bench, looking slightly sick.

But the snakes were so lovely he simply had to tell her about them, so every now and then he skipped across the room to describe the marvels she was missing. She seemed startled rather than pleased when he told her how the nice, kind man in charge of the show had actually let him hold a live snake in his hands.

48

"Don't worry, Mom, it was just a hog-nose adder—perfectly harmless," he assured her. "It was so cute—its tongue went in and out the whole time. Gosh, I sure do wish you could have seen me holding it."

It was nearly two hours before Bruce had looked his fill. When at last they were leaving the building he said regretfully,

"I do wish we had just a little more money, Mom, and that you liked snakes just a little bit better. They had some awfully nice ones for sale for only two or three dollars."

Lunch was ham-and-cheese sandwiches at a Liggett's soda fountain, followed by more ice cream—another chocolate soda for Bruce and a chocolate malted for his mother. When they had finished she said hopefully,

"Shall we go to the movies now, Bruce? We still have enough money for the Music Hall, if we hurry and get there before the afternoon prices start."

"Okay, I guess . . . Only I'll tell you what I'd rather do first, if you don't mind. I'd like to go to the 5-and-10-cent store, and just kind of look around. You know, you're generally in a hurry when we do go in one, and I never have looked around all I want to."

"Well . . . all right," said his mother, "if that's what you really want to do," and they walked to the nearest Woolworth's. It was a big new one, on two floors, and it took Bruce a long time to "look around." When he had examined everything thoroughly, and ridden up and down on the escalator for awhile, he remarked casually, "I'd like to spend about a million dollars here, wouldn't you, Mom?"

His mother looked in her coin purse. "You may have one toy, if it doesn't cost more than fifty cents," she said. Then, naturally, he had to "look around" all over again, to make sure of getting just what he wanted. After much deliberation he chose a toy water-pistol, and then he was ready to leave.

"Now what?" asked his mother wearily. The day had turned unexpectedly hot for early June, and her feet were beginning to hurt from so much walking. "Shall we go to a show now? We haven't enough money left for the Music Hall, but we could still go to one of the second-run movies on 42nd Street."

"Okay, the movies then," agreed Bruce, lovingly squishing the bulb of his new water-pistol. He was far too happy to walk beside his mother in the ordinary way, but hopped along on one leg, or ran backwards by spells, bumping into other pedestrians. As they approached the box office of a movie theatre on 42nd Street he stopped abruptly.

"Mom, wait! We forgot something important!"

"What?"

"Pounce. *We've* had ice cream, and a snake show, and everything, but we forgot to get a present for Pounce."

"Darling, don't be silly," said his mother, who, by this time, wanted very much indeed to sit down in a cool, dark movie and rest her feet. "All a kitten needs is enough to eat, and plenty of petting. There's nothing you can buy him for a present."

Bruce was a trifle crushed but unconvinced.

"Joanna's mother buys presents for their cats," he said gently, "lots of times. She gets them at a shop in Greenwich Village that has all kinds of stuff for cats."

"A shop for *cats*?"

"Yes. Joanna told me about it. I want to go there and buy a present for Pounce. Poor little Pounce, he ought to have some fun. Please, Mom."

His mother thought regretfully of the nice cool movie. "Well . . . it sounds absurd, Bruce, but if you really want to try to find this place . . ."

"Oh, I do!"

At a nearby drug store they looked in the classified telephone directory for the address of the shop. Somewhat to Mrs. Fleming's surprise it was actually listed, with a street number in Greenwich Village, just as Bruce had said. Again they took the subway and rode downtown to the Village, where, after a short walk, they found the place they were looking for. They knew at once that it was the right place, for, in the window, gazing serenely out into the street, was a tall black porcelain pussy cat.

Bruce rang the bell, and the door was opened by a slender dark-eyed woman who looked, somehow, rather like a cat herself, and who ushered them into the strangest shop they had ever seen.

It really was a shop just for cats. The walls were covered with pictures of cats and kittens, and everywhere you looked there were things for pussies that you would never have thought up by yourself. Wicker beds for cats, with soft cushions in them. Cunning little collars with bells on them, in red, blue, or green leather. Brightly colored bead necklaces, strung on elastic, so that a cat might slip out of one, if caught in a fence or hedge. Pretty dishes in all colors, shaped so that they could not tip over. Blankets, medicines, brushes and combs, claw-clippers, carriers for cats to travel in, and scratching posts for them to sharpen their claws on, instead of shredding the furniture. And toys, lots of toys, for cats and kittens to play with—catnip mice of gray flannelette, little celluloid balls that rattled enticingly, mechanical bugs that wound up and scuttled across the floor. And too many other things even to mention.

As they entered the shop a large gray-and-white cat jumped down from the counter and came to meet them. To the delight of the two customers he proceeded to help his mistress demonstrate the toys and equipment. He graciously allowed her to trim his claws with the claw-clipper, and to groom him with a brush and comb. When she opened a carrier he at once sprang inside, to show how well it fitted, and as she brought out each toy he reached a snowy forepaw and gave it an appreciative pat. Finally, as she was explaining the purpose of the scratching post, he stretched himself out long, and slowly and impressively sharpened his claws on it. Then he jumped back upon the counter, where he sat like a statue, patiently awaiting the next customer.

After examining everything Bruce decided upon a gray flannelette mouse, wrapped in cellophane, and a play-stick, to take to Pounce. The play-stick was a light wand with a red cord attached to it, ending in a tassel for a kitten to jump at.

"Are we going to the movies now?" he asked, when they were out on the street again.

"I'm afraid not," said his mother, "We haven't enough money left for a movie. We've got just—" she took out her coin purse and looked inside. "We've got just enough to get home on the subway, and a little over."

"I don't suppose we could have another soda at Schrafft's?"

"No, darling, we couldn't. But I'll tell you what we can do. We can walk on down to Washington Square, and if there's an ice cream wagon there we can each have a Good Humor, or an ice cream cone."

Bruce thought this a splendid idea, so they walked to Washington Square. Sure enough, there was a tinkling ice cream wagon, being pushed along by a white-clad Good Humor man, and followed by a crowd of eager children. Bruce and his mother each chose a delicious ice-cold chocolate Good Humor, wrapped in a little paper napkin. Sitting down on a bench they ate them carefully—as slowly as possible, to make the pleasure last, yet not *too* slowly, lest the ice cream suddenly melt off the stick, and—horrible thought—fall to the ground.

"You know, Mom," said Bruce, as he licked the last of the

ice cream from the little wooden stick, "I wish every day could be exactly like today, don't you? Wouldn't that be *perfect*?"

If his mother hesitated, it was only for a moment. "Of course it would, honey, and I'm awfully glad you have been so happy. And now we really must go, or we'll get caught in the subway rush, and have to stand up all the way home."

MALO

CHAPTER ELEVEN

Pounce knew their footsteps coming down the hall. They heard his funny little *"rarr"* before they opened the door, and when they entered the room there he was, perched on the foot of Mrs. Fleming's bed, waiting for them. He sprang to Bruce's shoulder and clung like a burr, sniffing his face lovingly and purring away like a small motor.

"Just you wait, Pouncie," cried Bruce. "You're going to have a surprise. Presents!" He tore open the package to show him the flannelette mouse and the play-stick.

"Look, Mom, look!" he exclaimed, as Pounce leapt for the

swinging red tassel. "I bet you never saw a kitten jump that high before!"

His mother did not answer. She didn't even look at them. She sat at her work table with her handbag open before her, and she was doing some kind of arithmetic on a piece of paper. She took out the thin folder of traveler's checks from the zipper compartment of her bag and counted them very carefully, twice. Then she just sat, looking straight in front of her.

"What's the matter, Mom? Why don't you look at Pounce? Have you got a headache or something?" Bruce was puzzled. His mother had been so nice all day, letting him have all that ice cream and everything, and now she was acting rather strange. He came and stood beside her, patting her shoulder.

"I'm sorry you didn't get to go to the movie," he said earnestly. "I guess you'd have liked it better than the snake show. Thanks for all the treats today, Mom."

His mother put her arm around him and began to talk rapidly.

"Bruce, I've something to tell you, and I may as well get it over with. I wish I could wait till morning, but that's no use, because I've got to start packing tonight, and you'd guess anyway."

"*Packing!*"

"Yes, we're leaving tomorrow. We're going home."

"But why, Mom? I thought you liked it here."

"Bruce, we've got to go home. We've used up all our money, and—"

"*All* of it?"

"All of it except just enough to get back to Portland on the bus."

"Well, that's okay, isn't it?" said Bruce. Then he remembered. Pounce couldn't go with them.

"Can we—can we take Pounce?" he faltered, although he knew the answer.

"Pounce will have to be given back to Joanna. She loves him and he'll have a happy home," said his mother gently. Bruce picked up the play-stick and began shaking it again, while tears ran down his cheeks.

His mother watched him for a few moments. Then she said, "I'd better go and call Mrs. Wiles now," and she went out to the telephone.

Bruce dropped the play-stick, and, throwing himself full length on the bed, began to sob. Pounce, puzzled by such behavior, sprang up on the bed beside him and patted his wet cheek with a soft forepaw. Bruce reached out blindly and drew the kitten to him. He buried his face in Pounce's warm fur and cried harder than ever.

After a while he sat up and rubbed his face with his hands. His mother was out in the hall, talking over the telephone, and he went to the door and listened. She seemed to be talking to

Mrs. Wiles, but how could she sound so cheerful? He heard her say,

"Why, yes, of course, Mrs. Wiles, I'd be glad to . . . Yes, practically any time . . . Tomorrow at eleven? That will be fine. Thank you so much. Goodbye."

She hung up the phone and turned eagerly to Bruce.

"Bruce, what do you think? Mr. and Mrs. Wiles liked those sketches of Joanna so much that they want me to do a portrait of her! Two portraits! They want one for themselves, and one to send to Mr. Wiles' parents in Michigan. And that isn't all. Mrs. Wiles works for a publishing company, and she says she's practically certain she can get me some book illustrating to do. I'm to take my drawings downtown tomorrow to her office. Isn't that *marvelous*?"

Bruce looked utterly bewildered.

"But—Pounce—are you going to give Pounce back to her?" he stammered. "Aren't we going to Portland on the bus, like you said?"

"Darling, don't you understand? We don't have to go back to Portland after all. Joanna's mother is going to help me find work here. We're going to stay right here in New York, and keep Pounce."

"Oh, Mom!" cried Bruce, "Do you *mean* it?" He grabbed her around the waist and gave her a hug. Then he picked up Pounce and hugged *him*. "Then everything is really okay?"

"Everything is really okay," said his mother.